D1032916

To
From
Date

Dedication

To Nita, Hunter, and Brent

I love the story that we walk together

Published by Worthy Inspired, a imprint of Worthy Publishing Group,
A division of Worthy Media, Inc.
One Franklin Park, 6100 Tower Circle, Suite 210, Franklin, TN 37067

Helping People Experience The Heart Of God

Library of Congress Control Number: 2013941853

ISBN 978-1-61795-812-0

Design and Illustration: ThinkpenDesign.com

Printed in China

1 2 3 4 5 6 7—RRD—20 19 18 17 16

A Walk One Winter Night

Al Andrews

www.worthyinspired.com

It was cold that winter evening as I ambled down my quiet street. I needed a walk to clear my mind of all the clutter and stress of this season.

SALE
50%

It seems that every year it gets worse. More obligatory parties. Irritated drivers and panicky shoppers.

Long lines everywhere.

I remember a time when I was more expectant; when the reason for all of this celebrating meant everything to me. But sadly, this night my internal monologue was, "Let's just get this thing over and get back to normal." Frankly, my cynicism troubled me. And when I am troubled, I take a walk.

Even if it's near midnight.

Even if it's cold.

Even if there are still

things to be done.

The hour was late and a light rain was falling. Stray flakes of snow twirled and mingled in. From windows and trees, the lights of the season sparkled through the heavy mist like stars aching to beam brightly on this dreary, dark night. Turning up my collar, I pulled my jacket tighter. That kind of cold finds its way through most any opening.

As I walked, I saw them out of the corner of my eye—Mary, Joseph, the baby Jesus—displayed in a wooden stable in someone's front yard. The usual characters were assembled as well—shepherds, sheep, a camel, and the wise men three. On the stable's roof, a precariously perched angel looked on and was tilting slightly to the left. All of them were illuminated by two bright floodlights shining from the grass in front of them.

I almost passed them by. They were easy to miss, as I've grown accustomed to their presence. They are, after all, available everywhere in all sizes—ornament size, mantle size, coffee table size, and yard size. They come in a box; easy to assemble.

But that night, and I'm not sure why, something caused me to turn my head, inviting me to linger. I stopped to look at them for a while as one would stand in front of a Rembrandt painting in a museum. I must admit, it felt somewhat odd and awkward. After all, grown-ups don't pause and stare at yard nativity scenes. But for some reason, that night, that moment, I felt I should be there.

To witness something.

To see.

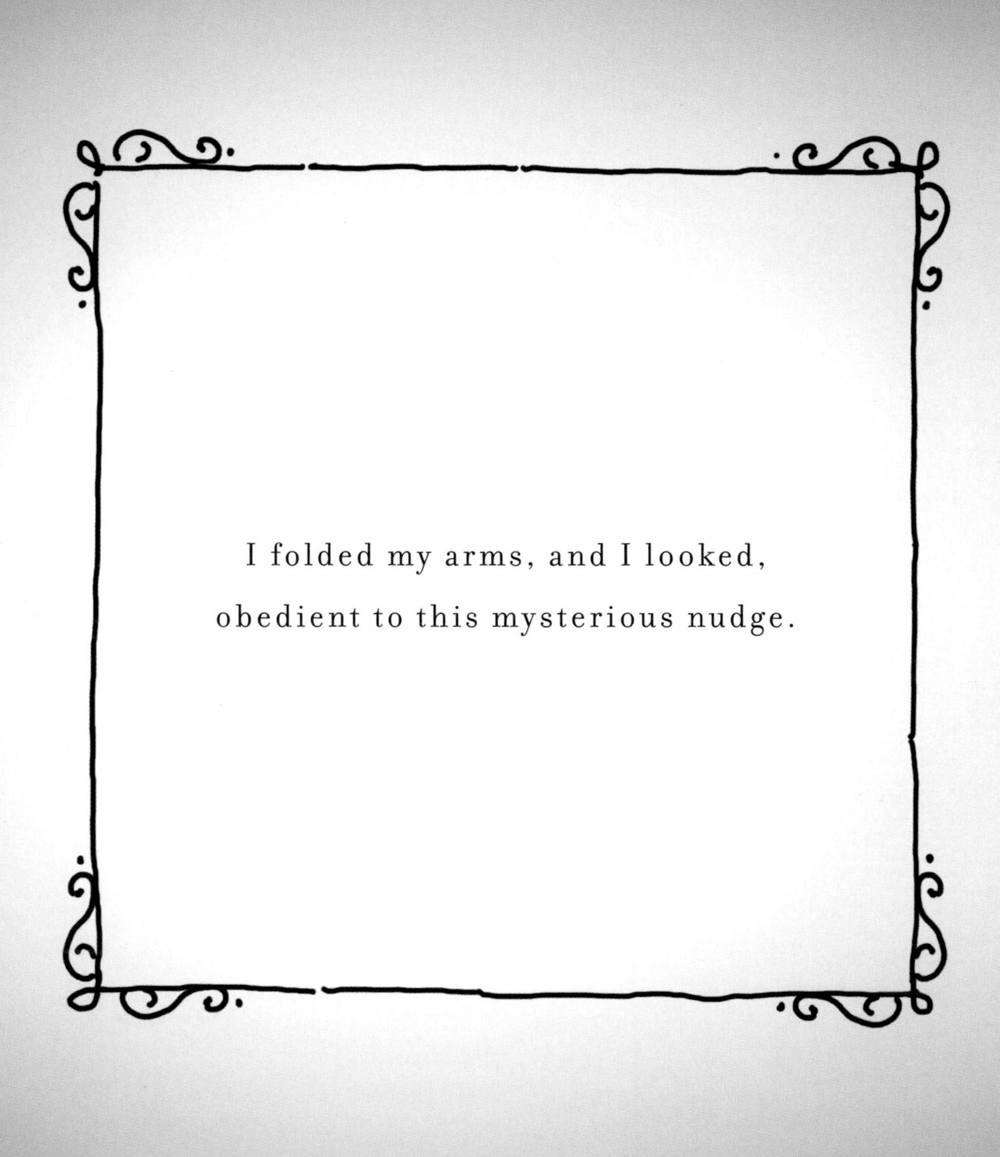

I folded my arms, and I looked,
obedient to this mysterious nudge.

She wore blue. Mary always wears blue. A neatly pressed, clean, blue garment. Her face, porcelain and untouchable, had a fixed expression, pleasant and peaceful. With her fragile hands folded in prayer, she gazed down adoringly at her child. She was perfect, this Mary—pristine, with moisture glistening on her smooth ceramic shawl.

Joseph wore brown. Joseph always wears brown. Brown is a fitting color for a character relegated to the background, for someone who never gets top billing. His eyes appeared vacant and his beard was neatly trimmed. He was there as he always is, on the edge. He can't seem to find his place. Everyone else has something distinctive—wings, crowns, gifts, halos, a shepherd's crook. But all he has is—brown.

Then there was the baby Jesus, his tiny arms extended. The star attraction. A halo encircled his little head—reaching from ear to ear. A clean white fabric wrapped around him. Swaddled, I suppose, is the appropriate Christmas word to use. He smiled an unearthly smile. He's always happy, this manger Jesus. It looked like he'd never slept and never cried. It didn't appear that he wanted to be held, nursed, or cuddled either.

I won't take the time to describe the others, but you know them well. You probably even know where each is positioned in the stable. The shepherds go there. The camels and sheep over there. The wise men—there, there, and there.

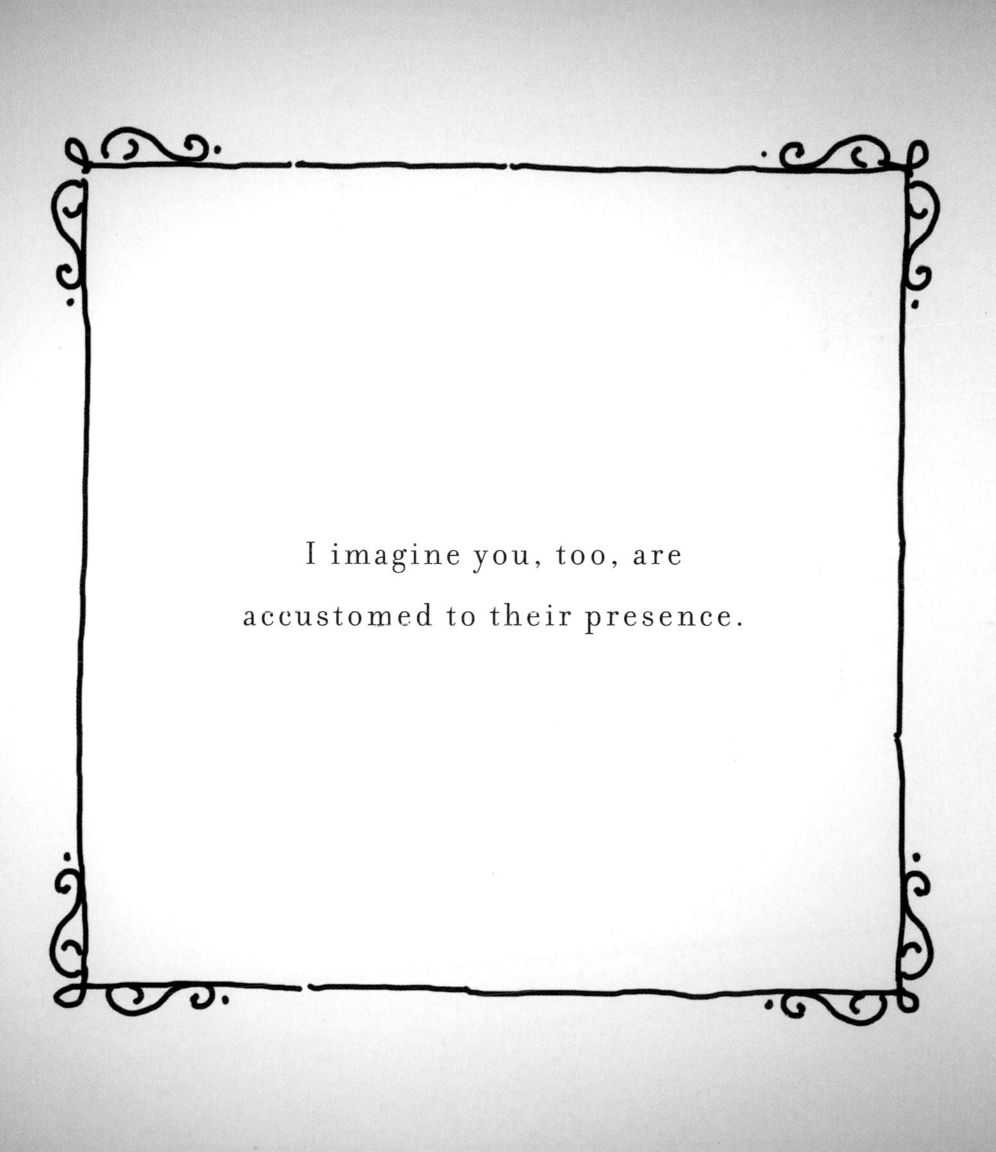

I imagine you, too, are
accustomed to their presence.

I remained standing, trying to stay warm. Looking at them through the gauzy mist, I pondered. I simply couldn't relate to them in any way. They seemed remote and untouchable, just like this season had become for me. With considerable guilt I wondered, "Why don't I like these people?"

After this abrupt and irreverent thought came to me, I half expected the ground underneath to open up and swallow me whole, or a bolt of lightning to descend with a flash and a snap, leaving a little pile of smoldering ashes that used to be me. I closed my eyes and waited for the end. Thankfully, neither the heavens nor the ground opened, so I continued my gaze.

And then something happened—something I frankly don't expect you to believe. I heard a noise coming from Mary's direction. It startled me. "Who's that?" I said. Though her figure didn't move, a soft voice pleaded, "This is not me," she cried. "This is not real," and her voice broke. "Please, listen to me."

“My garment—it isn’t this clean. And it’s not this brilliant shade of blue. It’s a blue faded by the dust of a long journey to Bethlehem. It smells of my sweat and of the mule whose back I rode upon. My blue is stained with red, the blood of birth. It’s soiled by the dung of a stable floor. And my face—my real face—is blemished. I am a teenage girl.”

“My brow is furrowed from worry. Worry about this baby, about tomorrow. What will Herod do? Will he find us? And my eyes. My eyes are red from tears of pain. I am so lonely and afraid. This is my first baby and my mother is not here with me. This is not who I am,” she said again. “I am real. Please, let me be real,” and her voice trailed off.

Her words, both gentle and
moving, reached inside of me so
deeply, I could barely breathe.
And while I was catching my
breath, I heard a deeper voice.

"You are wrong about me too." It was coming from Joseph's direction. "This is not me. This is not real. Please! Listen to me," he said firmly. I started to take a step backwards, but his voice riveted me in place.

"Listen," he repeated, "Really listen. I am not the quiet, simple character you make me out to be. My eyes are not vacant. Hours ago they were full of fire when I grabbed the innkeeper's tunic with a tight grip and said, 'Don't you tell me that there is not some room some where!' And he found a place for us."

"I am a man with a purpose—to travel where I was told to go, and to lead my family safely there. And we made it! Now that we are here, I am still on guard for we are in danger."

Joseph continued, "Yes, I wear brown, but it is for stealth. I blend in with my surroundings, and from my vantage point, my eyes scan every opening in this place for anyone who is out to do us harm. And no one will get by me. Let them try."

"I am the keeper of this light and I will keep him safe. You are wrong about me. This is not who I am. I am real. Please, let me be real." His words soaked into me like the evening's mist. I felt admonished and awakened to something that was true.

And then I heard a cry.

I looked at Jesus in the wooden manger. He was thrashing about in the hay. He had soiled himself and he looked uncomfortable. His cloth was twisted in his arms and legs. He grimaced from the prickly straw. His face was red and his cry grew louder, the cry of a hungry infant.

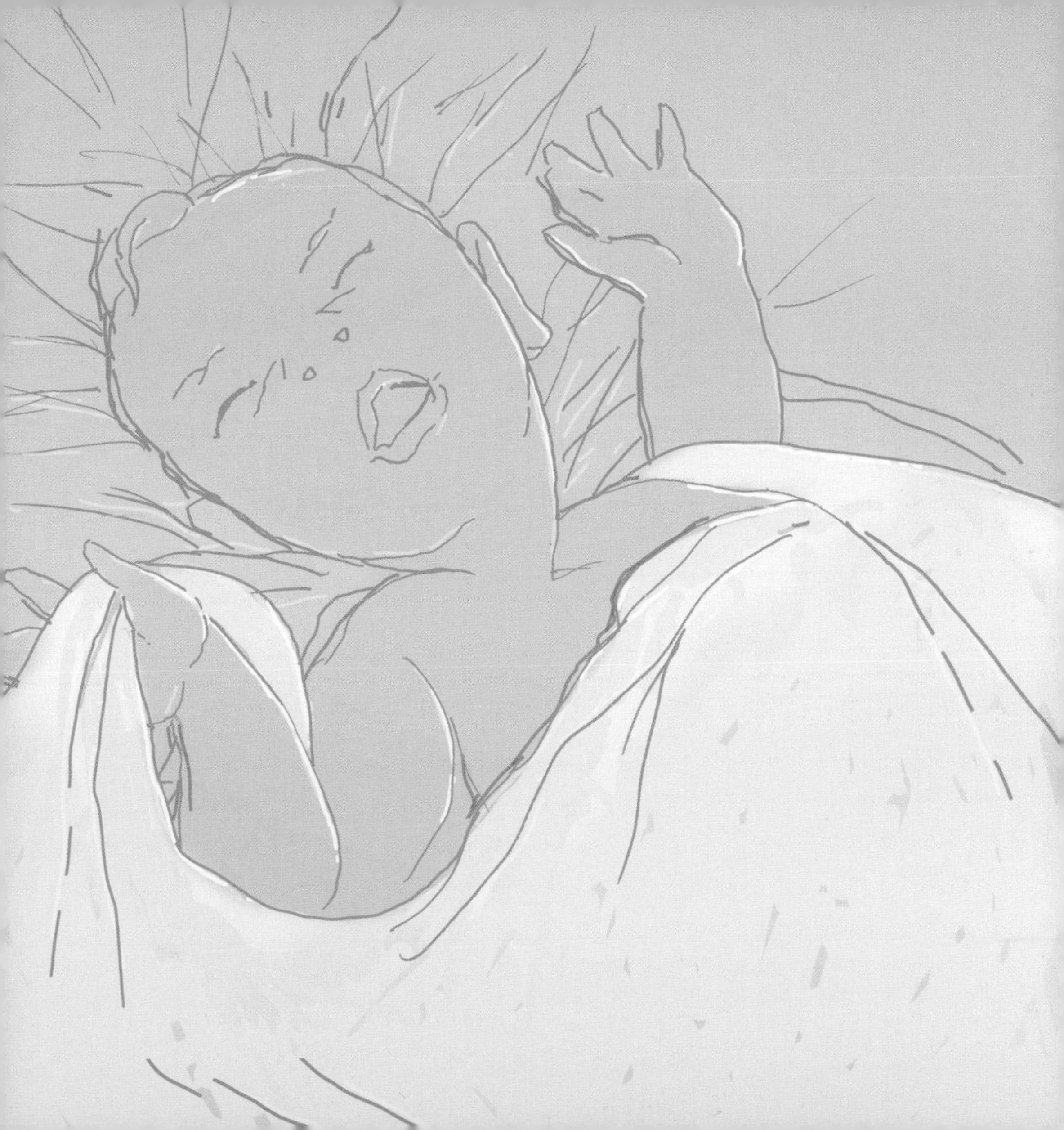

His toothless mouth opened and he arched his back. He cried so hard that he ran out of breath, and for a moment, it was quiet. But I knew it was the quiet before he drew another breath, and then he wailed so loudly I expected the lights in the nearby houses to turn on and the neighbors to come running out.

I wondered if he, too, would speak. But he didn't need to. Somehow his words were in me and I spoke for him. "This is not me. This is not real. Please, listen to me."

"The reason I came, the reason I was *sent*, was
to be *real*—to feel everything you've felt, to know
everything you need, because I needed it too.
To hurt like you've hurt, laugh like you've laughed,
skin my knee like you've skinned your knee,
and have my heart broken like your heart has been
broken. I came so that one day—or one winter
night, when you come face-to-face with your
defeat, your moment of absolute need, you
can come to me and say, 'You know this too.
Lead me through it.'

And I will."

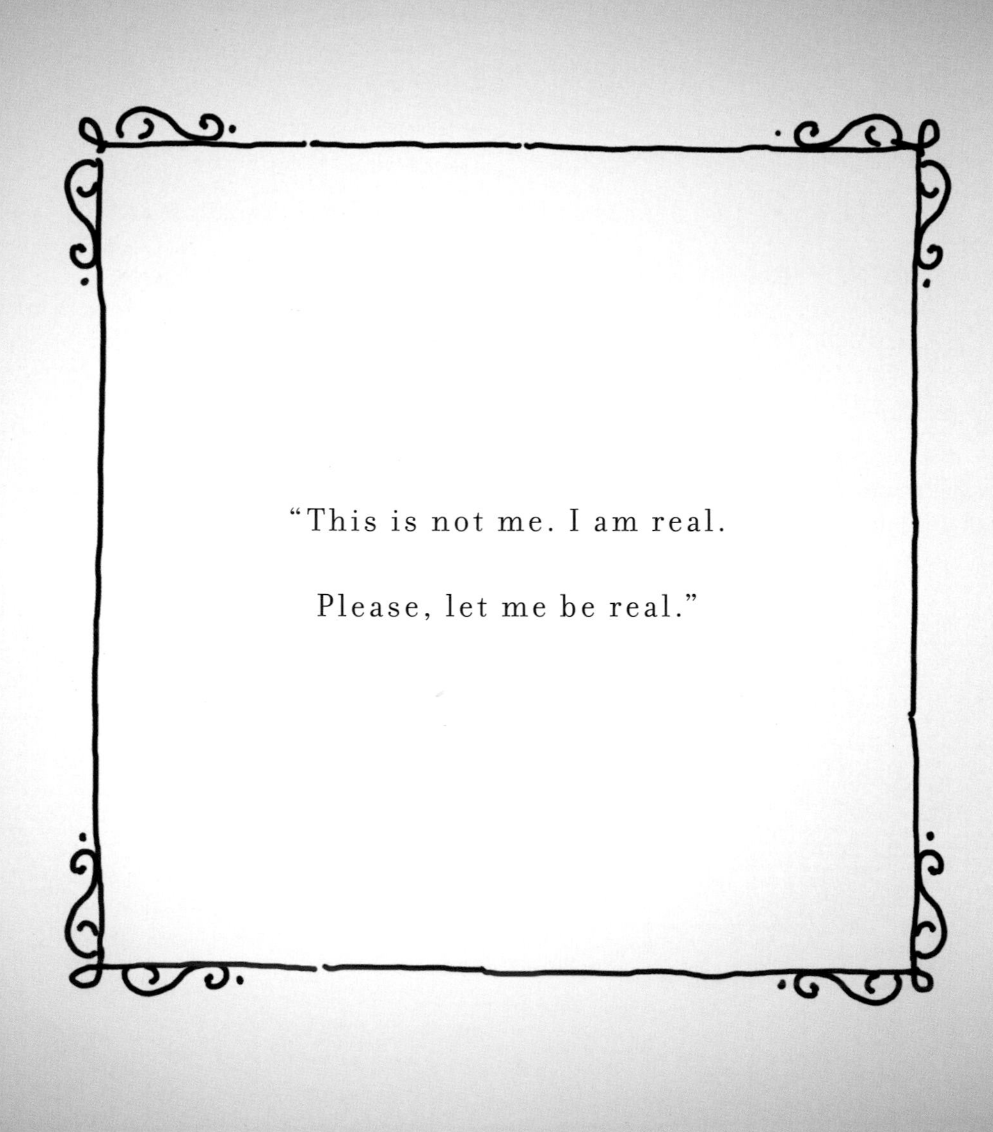
“This is not me. I am real.
Please, let me be real.”

Then there was silence—a long stillness that hushed the wind and pushed away the noises of the night. In the quiet, I was being given room—room to feel and consider what I'd just seen and heard. And out of the silence, the truth appeared like stars revealed by parting clouds.

Maybe the figures before me weren't real because I had made them that way so they would be predictable and safe, easy to ignore and box up after Christmas, out of sight and out of mind. Maybe if Jesus wasn't real, he would be tame and small. Maybe I had rendered Him untouchable, because I was afraid of his touch.

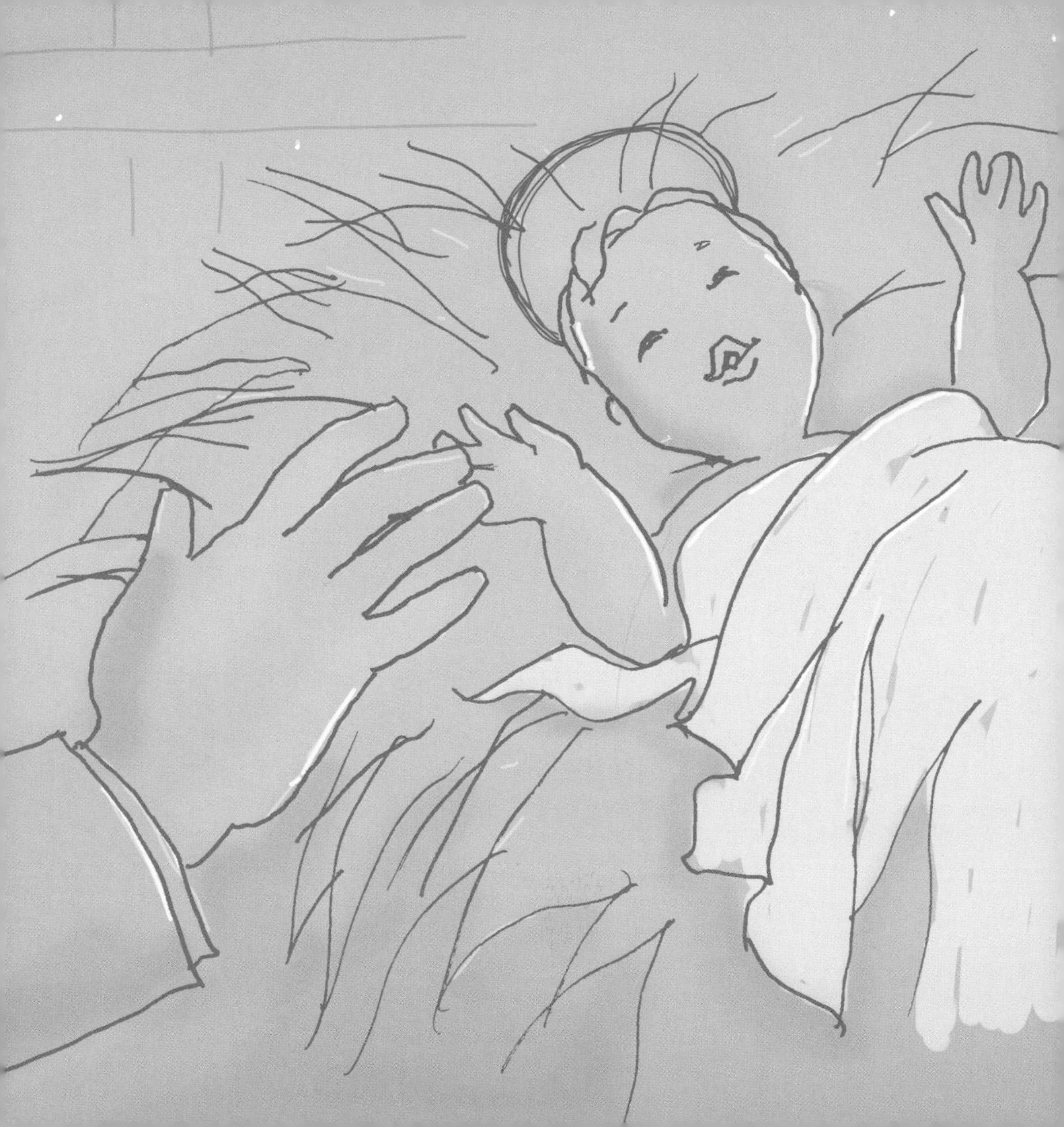

"I'm sorry," I said. "I know this isn't you. I can see it now. You're not who I've seen you to be—untouchable, perfect, something I made rather than someone who made me. You are real. You are true. You are here."

"I am so sorry," I said again as my eyes brimmed with tears. The sorrow nudged me to kneel next to a shepherd on the wet grass, in front of something so real, so very real, I couldn't even begin to comprehend it.

As I knelt, I became a part of the story and the story became a part of me, and I felt his gentle pardon. Suddenly, everything expanded—this scene, this night, my heart. And I felt...real.

I stood and remained there a while, quietly
looking at them as they gazed back at me.
And I realized something. I liked these
people now. And I think they liked me.

Shivering, I wondered if Jesus was cold too.
So I laid my scarf over his hands and his feet,
the same hands and feet I would one day see again.
I tucked him in as best I could. “Good night,”
I said to him. “Sleep well. You’ve traveled far.”

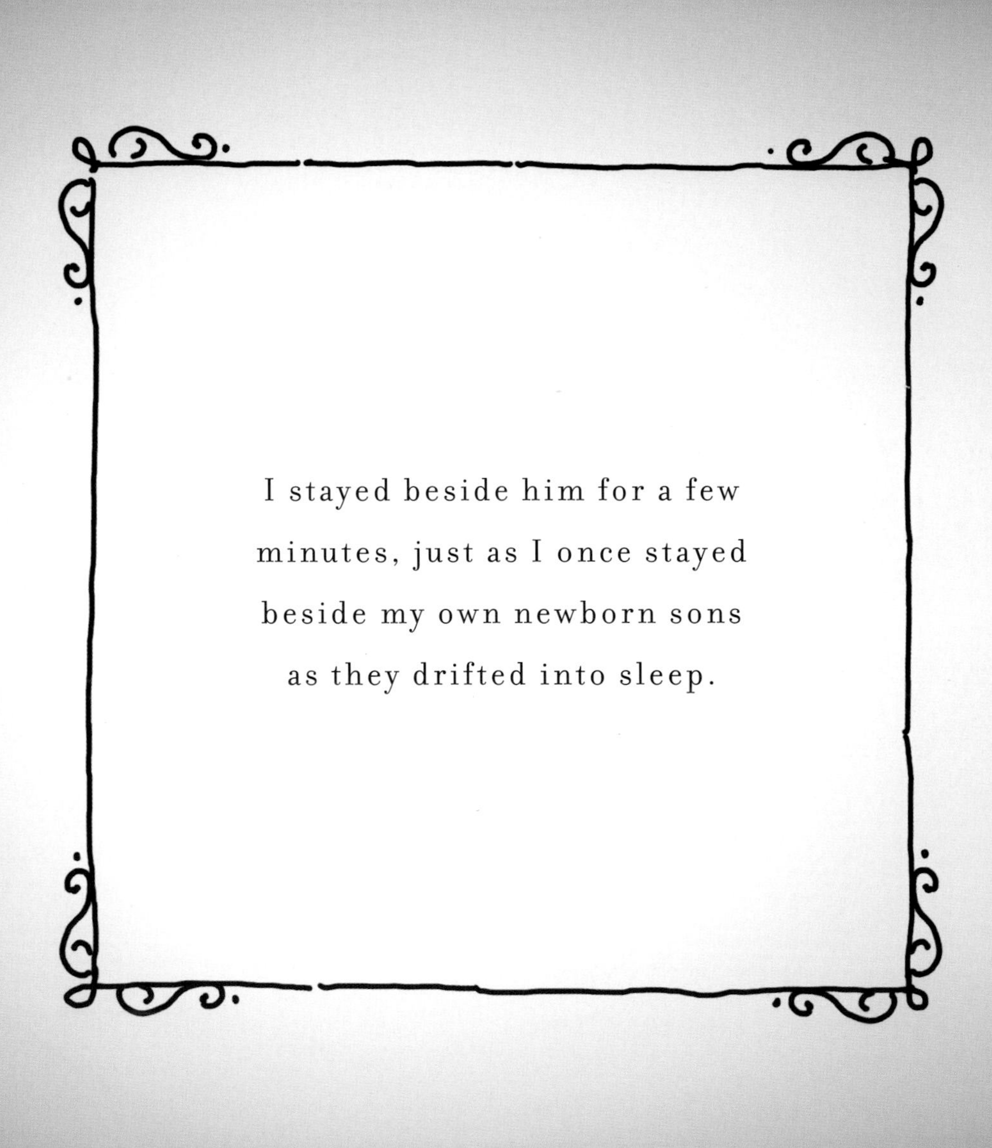

I stayed beside him for a few
minutes, just as I once stayed
beside my own newborn sons
as they drifted into sleep.

Then a low, regal voice came from one of the wise men. He whispered as if he was aware that Jesus was sleeping. "We, like you, were drawn to this place and have journeyed far to come here to see what you have seen. And what you have seen is what this world has been waiting for."

And from a shepherd standing behind Joseph, I heard another quiet voice. “Once you hear the angels sing, you will never be the same. If you listen carefully, they’re always singing.”

And then there was quiet. No more voices. No more movement. No more surprises. I sensed it was time to go.

I started the walk back to my house. The cold wind and a few flakes of snow urged me along. My pace was slow and thoughtful. This walk had become a journey I didn't want to end. Something had returned to me and I yearned for it to remain.

When I reached the corner of the street, I thought I heard singing and turned for one last look. In the distance, I saw a warm glow coming from a small wooden stable in a yard down the street, sheltering something inside that was older than the stars and bigger than our whole wide world.

And it was real.

Al Andrews is a counselor, author, and speaker. He is the founder and director of Porter's Call, a non-profit offering counsel, support, and encouragement to recording artists. He's a co-author of *The Silence of Adam* and wrote and self-published a children's book, *The Boy, the Kite, and the Wind.* Al lives in Nashville and is married to Nita. They have two sons.

Acknowledgements

With gratitude to Dave Barnes who commissioned this story for his 2011 Christmas concert at the Polk Theater in Nashville, TN, and to Bill Hearn who heard it and thought others should hear it too.

www.itsalandrews.com 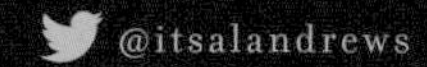 @itsalandrews